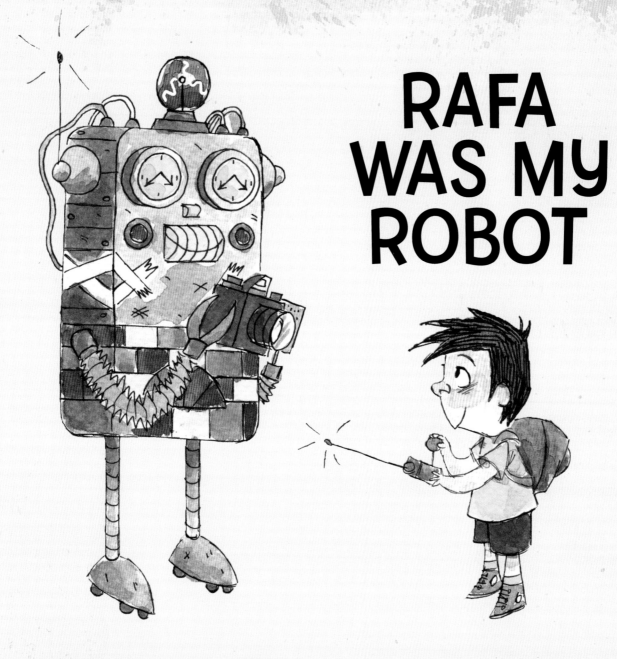

RAFA WAS MY ROBOT

By Alexandra Dellevoet • Art by Ken Turner

annick press
toronto + new york + vancouver

We acknowledge the support of the Canada Council for the Arts, the Ontario Arts Council, and
the Government of Canada through the Canada Book Fund (CBF) for our publishing activities.

ONTARIO ARTS COUNCIL
CONSEIL DES ARTS DE L'ONTARIO
50 YEARS OF ONTARIO GOVERNMENT SUPPORT OF THE ARTS
50 ANS DE SOUTIEN DU GOUVERNEMENT DE L'ONTARIO AUX ARTS

Cataloging in Publication

Dellevoet, Alexandra, author
     Rafa was my robot / Alexandra Dellevoet ; art by Ken Turner.

Issued in print and electronic formats.
ISBN 978-1-55451-679-7 (bound).—ISBN 978-1-55451-678-0 (pbk.).—
ISBN 978-1-55451-681-0 (pdf).—ISBN 978-1-55451-680-3 (epub)

     I. Turner, Ken (Ken A.), illustrator II. Title.

PS8607.E48755R33 2014   jC813'.6   C2014-900176-2
                                                 C2014-900177-0

Distributed in Canada by: Published in the U.S.A. by Annick Press (U.S.) Ltd.
Firefly Books Ltd.   Distributed in the U.S.A. by:
50 Staples Avenue, Unit 1   Firefly Books (U.S.) Inc.
Richmond Hill, ON L4B 0A7   P.O. Box 1338
                                   Ellicott Station
                                   Buffalo, NY 14205

Printed in China

Visit us at: www.annickpress.com
Visit Alexandra Dellevoet at: www.alexdellevoet.com
Visit Ken Turner at: kenturner.blogspot.ca

Also available in e-book format. Please visit www.annickpress.com/ebooks.html for more details.
Or scan

To Theo,
Jacob,
Nancy,
Ian, and
Heather.

A Note from the Author

A dear friend of mine, Norm Ringel, passed away in May of 2011. Before his departure from this world, one of
his prime concerns was for his eight-year-old nephew and how grief might affect him. I personally researched
children's books on the subject of loss and found very few options. And so, the story of *Rafa Was My Robot* was born.
I hope that this book will be a help to parents, guardians, and all people who are dealing with children who have lost
a loved one—whether it is a robot, pet, friend, or family member. Death is difficult for adults to navigate, and even
more so for young children.

Rafa was a robot built out of scraps and a whole lot of love.

Jacob took Rafa everywhere. To swim lessons,

to school,

to Paris,

to Stockholm,

to meet Norman the doorman,

and even to a faraway galaxy.

Then one day Rafa didn't feel so hot.

So Jacob took him to see the doctor.

The doctor said Rafa was running out of juice.

So Jacob ran out and bought all the juice he could find.

When he returned, the
doctor said, "Not that kind
of juice, this kind of juice."
And he held up one of
Rafa's batteries, which
needed replacing.

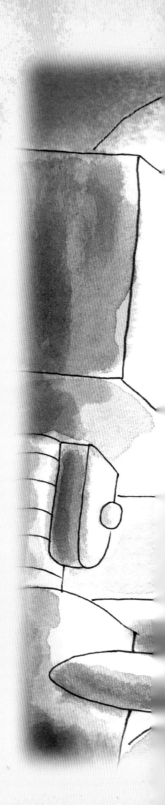

Jacob traveled the
world looking for this
special battery. He was
worried and scared and
somehow knew that he
had to hurry.

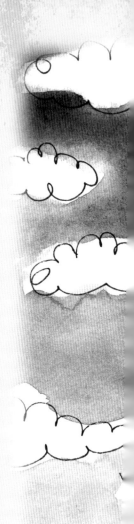

Meanwhile, night after night, Rafa
waited for Jacob to return.

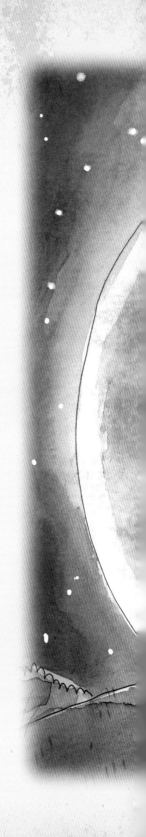

Jacob turned the world upside down looking for the battery.

At the end of every day he scribbled a postcard to Rafa sharing with him a few details from his search.

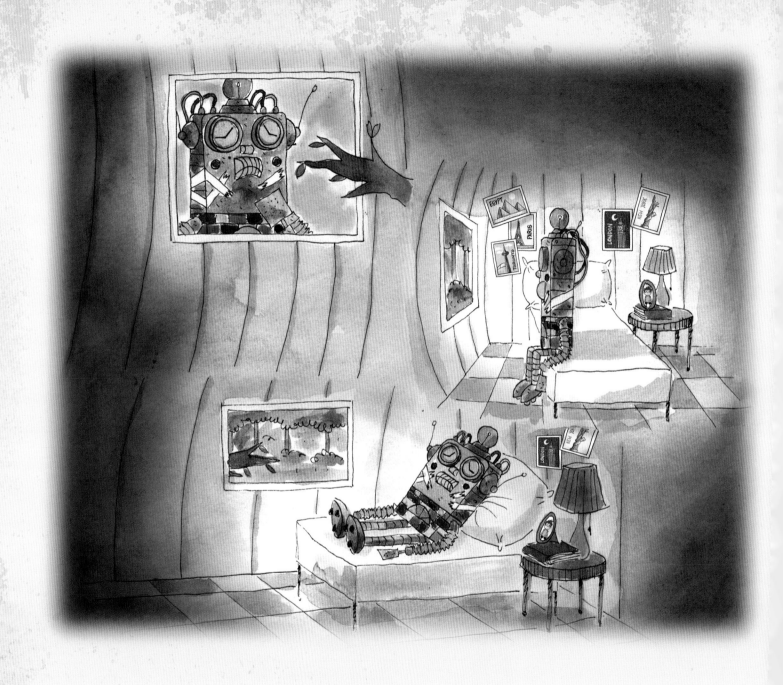

And as each day passed, Rafa became weaker and weaker.

Finally Jacob returned home. Only he was empty-handed.

Jacob held Rafa's hand and said, "The battery is a one-of-a-kind—just like you." They sat peacefully together for a long moment. When Jacob looked up, Rafa had died.

Jacob cried and cried and cried, until he filled the tub with all his sadness. He wondered how he would go on without Rafa.

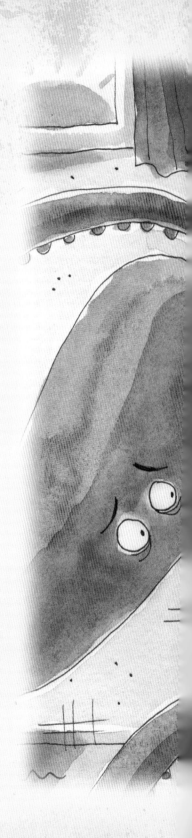

Jacob buried Rafa in the garden with the flowers and snails. He piled some rocks high and made a special place where he could visit Rafa every day.

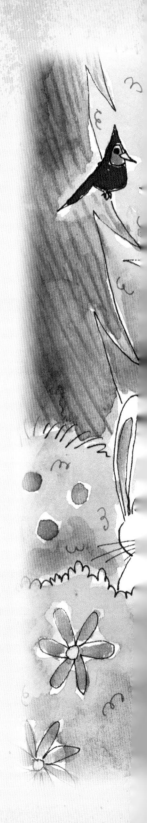

Jacob also made a pillow with a picture
of Rafa on it. He took it to bed with him
every night. And every night before going
to sleep he whispered to his pillow,
"If I don't meet you today, then I'll
meet you tonight. In my dreams."

Sweet dreams ...